PICK-UP BASKETBALL

CRAIG ELLENPORT

The Child's World®
childsworld.com

Published by The Child's World®
1980 Lookout Drive • Mankato, MN 56003-1705
800-599-READ • www.childsworld.com

Photo Credits
© 2xSamara.com/Shutterstock.com: 10; age
fotostock/Alamy Stock Photo:14; Gabriele Maltinti/
Shutterstock.com: 13; Gennadiy Titkov/Shutterstock.
com: 5; Sergey Novikov/Shutterstock.com: 6-7,
9, 21; Serrnovik/Dreamstime/Dreamstime: cover;
Wikimedia: 17; Zeljko Dangubic/Dreamstime:18

ISBN: 9781503823686
LCCN: 2017944892

Printed in the United States of America
PA02356

ABOUT THE AUTHOR

Craig Ellenport is a sportswriter from New York. He has written for USA Basketball's official website and works for the BIG3, Ice Cube's professional 3-on-3 basketball league.

TABLE OF CONTENTS

HOOP IT UP!

To play "pick-up" is to play an unplanned game. It is time to play pick-up basketball!

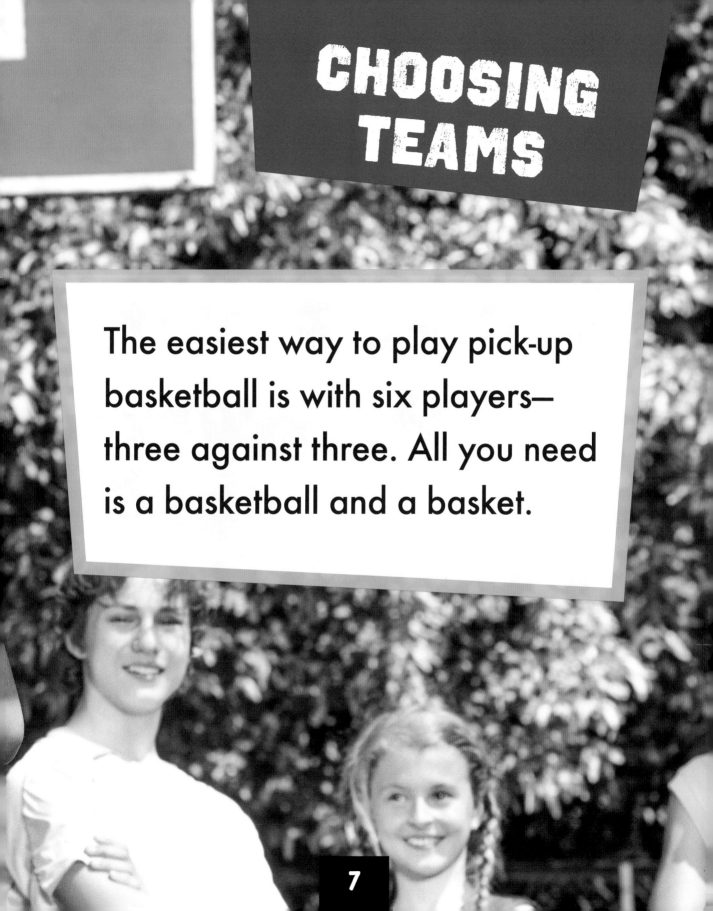

CHOOSING TEAMS

The easiest way to play pick-up basketball is with six players— three against three. All you need is a basketball and a basket.

GAME ON!

One team starts with the ball. They are on **offense**. Players move the ball by **dribbling** and passing. Points are scored by throwing the ball into the hoop.

FUN FACT

Around the world, 3-on-3 is a very popular form of basketball. On June 9, 2017, 3-on-3 basketball became an official Olympic sport.

FUN FACT

In 2017, the actor Ice Cube cofounded the BIG3, a 3-on-3 basketball league with former NBA players.

There are three things you can do with the basketball in your hand. You can take a shot, you can pass the ball to a teammate, or you can dribble.

When a player dribbles all the way up to the basket and takes a shot as they are jumping, that is called a **layup**.

When you are farther away from the basket, use a jump shot. Stop dribbling and hold the ball near your head. As you jump, push the ball up. Try to make the ball spin backward as you aim at the basket.

FUN FACT

The most famous court for pickup basketball games might be Rucker Park in New York City. Many great players got their start at Rucker Park before going on to the NBA, and there was even a TV show made about Rucker Park, called "On Hallowed Ground."

DEFENSE

The team that does not have the ball is on **defense**. There are two types of defense. In **man-to-man defense**, each player is assigned to cover a player from the other team.

In **zone defense**, each player is in charge of one area, or zone, on the court. Players cover any other players who enter that zone.

FUN FACT

These three players are each covering a zone on the court.

FUN FACT

Elmore Smith holds the NBA record with 17 blocked shots in a game in 1973.

HANDS UP

It is important for players on defense to keep their hands up. That way they can block a pass or a shot. If the defense gets the ball back without the other team scoring, that is called a **turnover**. Now *that* team is on offense!

FOR THE WIN!

When a basket is made, the other team gets the ball. Each basket in pick-up basketball is worth one point. Play until one team scores 21 points. Then it is time to shake hands. Good game!

FUN FACT

In most pick-up games, you have to win by two points or more. So if you're playing to 21 and the score is 20-20, that means now the teams must play to 22!

GLOSSARY

defense (DEE-fenss): The team that is trying to stop the team with the ball from scoring is on defense.

dribble (DRIB-ull): The way a player moves from place to place with a basketball. Players must bounce the ball with one hand the whole time they are running or walking.

layup (LAY-up): A way to shoot a basketball on the run. The player holds the ball in one hand, jumps up with the opposite leg, and throws the ball while in the air.

man-to-man defense (MAN TO MAN DEE-fenss): A game plan in which each player covers a single player on the other team.

offense (OFF-enss): The team with the ball (that is trying to score) is on offense.

professional (pruh-FESH-uh-null): A professional athlete is a person who plays a sport for money.

turnover (TURN-oh-vur): When the ball switches from one team to the other during a play, it is called a turnover.

zone defense (ZOHN DEE-fenss): A game plan in which players cover an area of the court.

TO LEARN MORE

In the Library

Campbell, Forest G., and Fred Ramen. *An Insider's Guide to Basketball*. New York, NY: Rosen Central, 2015.

Kaplan, Bobby. *Bball Basics for Kids: A Basketball Handbook by Bobby Kaplan*. Bloomington, IN: iUniverse, 2012.

Sports Illustrated for Kids, eds. *Sports Illustrated Kids Slam Dunk!: Top 10 Lists of Everything in Basketball*. New York, NY: Time Home Entertainment, 2014.

On the Web

Visit our Web page for lots of links
about pick-up basketball:

childsworld.com/links

Note to parents, teachers, and librarians: We routinely verify our Web links to make sure they are safe, active sites—so encourage your readers to check them out!

INDEX